MR. MEN
HALLOWEEN PARTY

Roger Hargreaves

Original concept by
Roger Hargreaves

Written and illustrated by
Adam Hargreaves

EGMONT

Mr Happy had decided to have a fancy dress Halloween party.

A trick or treat party.

He spent a whole day decorating his house.

He hung bats and spiders from the ceiling and cobwebs from lanterns.

There were creepy crawlies on the walls and a witch in the fireplace.

Mr Happy spent all afternoon carving as many gruesome-looking pumpkins as he could find.

Two of them looked rather familiar.

By the time the guests started to arrive, the garden was covered with glowing pumpkins.

Mr Happy dressed up as a vampire to greet his friends.

Little Miss Magic dressed up as a witch and arrived on a flying broomstick.

Mr Bump looked like he had dressed up as a mummy, but actually he had just had a lot more bumps that day than usual.

And there was someone dressed as a ghost, but nobody could work out who it was under the sheet.

Mr Happy had laid a whole table of treats for everyone and a black cauldron full of fizzy drink.

There was green jelly slime, strawberry jam blood sandwiches, meringue ghosts and gingerbread skulls.

There were games to play as well.

Like bobbing for apples.

Mr Noisy won easily.

Well, he does have a very big mouth.

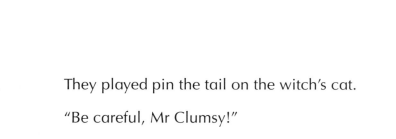

They played pin the tail on the witch's cat.

"Be careful, Mr Clumsy!"

And they all admired each other's costumes.

Mr Nosey was very curious to know who the ghost was.

"Go on then," he said to the ghost, "I give up, who are you?"

Wordlessly, the ghost rose up into the air.

Little Miss Giggles giggled nervously.

"Oh my," she squeaked. "It's a real ghost!"

"Don't be silly," snorted Mr Uppity. "There's no such thing."

The ghost laughed an eerie hollow laugh and rattled its chains.

Everyone looked scared.

But not as scared as when they saw the ghost walk through the wall!

There was just the sheet left!

There was no one there.

Mr Brave screamed a high-pitched scream.

And then suddenly Mr Impossible appeared out of nowhere.

"My goodness," laughed Mr Happy. "That was quite some Halloween trick. You really had us scared!"

"I wasn't scared," huffed Mr Uppity, as he crawled out from under the table.

"That was a clever disappearing trick," said Little Miss Tiny.

"Yes, nearly as clever as that disappearing trick!" exclaimed Mr Impossible, pointing to the table.

The table that had been covered with treats.

The table that was now empty.

The table that Mr Greedy was standing beside!

A rather guilty-looking Mr Greedy.

A Mr Greedy who couldn't help himself.

A Mr Greedy with a monster appetite!